This book is given with love:

For all inquiries, please contact us at:
info@puppysmiles.org

To see more of our books, visit us at:
www.PuppyDogsAndIceCream.com

— THE GREAT —
BEAR BRIGADE
LOST IN THE WOODS

Written By:
Jason Kutasi

Illustrated by:
Javier Gimenez Ratti

The Great Bear Brigade has lots of stories to share.
  Once you read their adventures then you'll be aware,
Of life lessons to learn and how to take care.
  They will help you live smart and always beware!

It's a really cool hike,
when you get to play scout...

When you know the way home,
and can figure it out.

But the trail can be scary,
and fill you with doubt...

When you're lost in the woods,
no one can hear you shout.

You should always think twice,
before climbing trees...

You might grab a branch,
and stir up some bees.

The Brigade knows the forest,
and roams it with ease...

There are tricks they can share,
if you just ask them please.

Before you get frightened,
and start losing your mind...

The Bear Brigade will come,
to get you out of your bind.

Remember their suggestions,
which might help you find...

The quickest way back,
so you aren't left behind.

When you and your friends,
go off hunting for treasure...

Tell someone where you're going,
and take a map for good measure.

Have a plan to get home,
without any pressure...

Knowing the directions,
will make it a pleasure.

The Great Bear Brigade is simply the best.
When they sense you're in trouble, they'll never rest,
And all of their skills will be put to the test.
They're happy to help, and they do it with zest!